WARNING

This book contains sexually explicit scenes and adult language. It may be considered offensive to some readers. This book is for sale to adults ONLY.

* * * * * * * * * * * * * * * * * *

Please store your files wisely where they cannot be accessed by underage readers.

ISBN-13: 978-1987863727
ISBN-10: 1987863720

Other books by Shyla Starr:

<u>Persuasive Billionaire BWWM Romance Series</u>

Stacey is trying to keep a handle on her life the best that she can. She is on the verge of losing her job and her apartment, while taking care of her sick grandmother. Her life takes an unexpected turn when she meets Charlie, who works for the construction company that is attempting to persuade her to move out of her home.

<u>Tenacious Billionaire BWWM Romance Series</u>

Adalia is too proud to accept help from the billionaire playboy, Trent Dawson. How long can she maintain her resolve? The bank is at her heels to repossess her business. To make matters worse, Adalia finds suspicious evidence of Trent's philandering ways. She must determine whether to trust Trent with the fate of her business and her heart.

<u>Elusive Billionaire Romance Series</u>

Billionaire Hendrick is trying to repair his company's image by putting in some volunteer work, building a school and hospital for the impoverished children in Africa. There, he meets a beautiful African American volunteer, Jocelyn. They hit it off right away but does she belong in his world?

<u>Lonely Billionaire Romance Series</u>

Tricia was hired to care for billionaire John's wife, who is dying. An unlikely romance emerges after his wife, Rebecca, gives John permission to pursue his happiness after she is gone.

<u>Ardent Billionaire Romance Series</u>

Deirdre doesn't know what to make of the gorgeous man that seems to be interested in her. His name is Parker Walters and he seems friendly enough. There is just something off about him. Why is he trying the hide the fact that he is the heir to his father's billion dollar software empire?

<u>Fervent Billionaire BWWM Romance Series</u>

Alexandra had never been with a white man before. She had seen William at the café before but she always kept her distance. It was unfortunate that their first chance meeting happened when she dropped her breakfast and spilled coffee all over his expensive business suit.

Get the latest update on new releases from the author at:

https://shylastarr.com/newsletter/

This book is Part Three of the "Audacious Billionaire BWWM Romance Series"

1 - Love Eluded

Chante is torn between staying close to a man beyond her league, and fleeing from him to spare herself from a hopeless position. But she finds she is propelled into a place where she needs to confront her doubts and cast her fate aside to follow the dictates of her heart. Damned if she does and miserable is she doesn't, how will Chante face the events that will lead her to a place of pure happiness or to the pits of a broken heart?

2 - Love Astray

Chante is slowly getting over her heartbreak from the enigmatic Jared Lowell. Realizing that he is not the right man for her, she is ready to fall in love again and finds happiness once more in the arms of her new lover, Dr. Leo Cadman. That is until Jared's presence at the hospital stirs up all the emotions she used to have for him. Torn between the affections of a man who adores her and a sexual attraction she cannot contradict, who will Chante gamble her heart with?

3 - Love Abided

Chante finds herself accepting a marriage proposal from a man everybody considers 'the perfect man'. She knows she is the luckiest woman on earth. But although she could fool everyone else, she could never fool herself. Her heart belongs to Jared Lowell. It always had since the day she first laid eyes on him. Caught between a farce of an engagement and a growing

intimacy between her and Jared, which will win in the
battle for the truth... her heart or her mind?

Audacious Billionaire BWWM Romance Series

Love Abided

Book Three

By Shyla Starr

Table of Contents

Chapter One

IT HAS been three weeks since the marriage proposal and Chante knew what she had to do. She knew it since the night she said 'yes' to Dr. Leo Cadman. Her sense of right and wrong had been bothering her like crazy since. It wasn't like she didn't have feelings for Leo. In her heart there was a special place for him. Even her common sense was telling her she did the right thing in accepting the ring. But how could she deny the little nagging voice telling her she was a fraud?

If it were just her and Leo in the equation, the conclusion would be a given. There was no doubt that he was the perfect man for her. She could learn to love him totally. But the existence of one Jared Lowell made the equation more complex than it should have been.

Considering that Jared hasn't even hinted about his true feelings- or any feeling for that matter- about her, Chante thought she was awfully stupid to feel guilty about accepting Leo's marriage proposal.

Couldn't she just consider Jared an infatuation and move on with her 'happily ever after' with an eligible doctor who obviously was crazy in love with her?

She knew the answer. If she was really honest with herself, she knew it all along. It wasn't like a bolt of lightning that just came out of the blue. She was in love with Jared and she had to tell Leo the truth. Whatever the consequences or outcome about her decision, she had to do it soon.

The engagement ring he had given her lay heavily in her left hand ring finger. She shouldn't even have worn it out onto the streets. The single solitaire diamond reflected the light from the street lamps she passed by.

She spotted a small café, entered the premises and sat at a barstool. The bar of the café faced a glass mirror looking out into the street. It was a small dive compared to the more glitzy ones but it was in Queens and near the home she shared with her brother, Markey. His sleeping meds had taken effect almost immediately and Chante took the time to go out into the fresh air and think about her dilemma.

Droplets of rain cascaded down the glass window as Chante let out a sigh of frustration.

"Swell…" she muttered under her breath.

Even the weather was a reflection of the guilt in her heart. It was a good thing Leo was gone for the entire week. He had to attend a medical conference in Atlanta, giving Chante precious time to work out how she would handle the situation when he came back. Initially he was hesitant to leave so soon after the proposal. He wanted to spend as much time as he could with her but Chante reassured him it was fine. The medical conference was a step forward in his career as an ER doctor.

But even Chante understood why she wanted him away. It would give her time to put her thoughts into perspective and she could only do that if she wasn't feeling so guilty about him being around her all the time.

She had to break the engagement. It wasn't fair to the guy. How could she pretend to love him when she knew that her feelings didn't go deep enough to deserve the ring he had given her?

And Jared was gone too. He left word that he would be gone for a few days to attend to some personal concerns. That left Chante feeling gloomy and abandoned, but also relieved that he didn't have to know about her current status – engaged to Dr. Leo Cadman.

She was hoping that by the time Jared got back, if he ever came back at all, she would have untangled herself from this farce of an engagement.

Right now, she felt trapped between a rock and a hard place, but one thing was for sure, she had to break an engagement that she was sure she couldn't live up to.

She probably would end up alone and miserable just the same, but at least her conscience wouldn't be nagging her day and night.

Chante ordered a beer and nursed her drink. She glanced at her watch and decided to drink up and head for home. The rain was now just a drizzle and she could sprint the few blocks home.

She pulled out her purse to pay the bill when a familiar voice greeted her.

"Well-well-well, if it isn't my favorite girl. Fancy meeting you here." The voice sneered.

Chante whirled swiftly around, a sudden fear creeping into her heart. She knew that voice.

"Oh… hi Jimmy…" Chante addressed him with a squeaky voice.

The new arrival was Jimmy Derollo, her ex-boyfriend. The guy always gave her the creeps. Chante wondered what she ever saw in him. Even now as he sidled towards her in the bar, she felt her skin crawl and the hair on the back of her neck stand on end.

Their last confrontation weeks ago on the sidewalk while waiting for the bus was something Chante wanted to forget. The hard slap she gave him on the face after he tried to kiss her still resounded in her ear. She vaguely remembered the threat he made as she swiftly boarded the bus. But she couldn't forget the murderous look in his eyes as the bus pulled away from him.

The bar was half-full and Chante knew that Jimmy wouldn't try anything stupid. One scream and even the bartender would probably come to her rescue. Still…she wasn't sure if she could deal with him once she was outside the confines of the bar. He could follow her home and she came alone.

No…Chante decided her best defense was to play it nice. Maybe if she played her cards well, he would leave her alone.

"Jimmy," she said again as he took the barstool next to hers and coolly ordered a glass of beer.

Jimmy turned his head and eyed her. Chante was uncomfortable with the way his eyes travelled up and down her body. She decided to ignore it remembering that she needed to keep her wits about.

Jimmy took a slug from the mug that left froth around his upper lip. Chante fought the urge to cringe with distaste. The glint in his eyes scared her. But fear was one the things that she didn't want him to see. Guys like Jimmy Derollo were bullies and fear only made him more potent and dangerous.

"I'll cut to the chase, bitch…" Jimmy said in a low voice, "I need some money and you will give it to me."

"What?" Chante asked in shocked surprise, "what the fuck makes you think that I will give you…"

Her shock had turned to irritation and it showed in her voice.

"Oh…but you will," Jimmy replied in a cold voice, whipping out a cell phone from his back pocket.

Chante wondered what he meant and was confused. Jimmy was scrolling through his phone until he found what he was looking for.

"You and I…we made a movie together. You probably don't remember because you were fucking high out of your mind. But here…watch…," Jimmy said as he handed her the phone.

Chante took the phone from his hand as Jimmy pressed the 'play' button.

Chante watched in horror as the video ran. The position was moving unevenly as a hand held out the phone from a distance, but there was no mistaking the images in the video. It was her and Jimmy fucking the hell out of her. She knew she was unconscious when it was taken but anyone seeing it would think she had her eyes closed in ecstasy.

Chante dropped the phone as Jimmy caught it in his hand and placed it back inside his pocket.

"As I was saying…I need some money, or else…" He taunted her.

"Or else what…" Chante asked, the words coming out of her mouth with some difficulty.

"Oh you know… I could upload it to the hospital website. I'm sure the hospital bigwigs would be so happy to know that one of their nurses is such a slut." Jimmy said.

Chante was dumbfounded. She couldn't believe what she was hearing. He was blackmailing her with a video he took without her knowledge and she was helpless to do anything about it. She couldn't speak.

The shock of seeing the images on the video turned her face gray with fear.

Suddenly her whole world was spinning around her. Everything turned black and she had to conquer the feeling of nausea that was threatening to overcome her. She grasped the edge of the bar to keep from falling.

"Jim-Jimmy, I-I-I'm not even a nurse…I'm an assistant nurse… and the little I earn go to the needs of Markey. You know that. Please-please, don't do this to me." Chante found herself begging.

She had a few bills in her purse and she felt dismally pathetic as she scooped it out and handed it to him.

Jimmy gave a chilling laugh as he pushed back her hand. He was enjoying himself immensely.

"Stupid cunt, you think I will accept loose change?" he asked.

And then he added, "You have access to the hospital pharmacy, right? So…why don't you grab a few bottles of them drugs and sell them to make money, right? A few thousand…Or-or you can sell that ring on your finger. Then your secret's safe with me."

Chante was horrified at what he was suggesting.

"Jimmy…that's impossible…I-I-can't do that." she replied.

Jimmy stared at her as if she were the village idiot who couldn't comprehend what he was saying. Then the murderous look returned into his eyes.

"Fucking whore…I don't care where you get the money as long as you get it, ok? Three days from today. Or the whole world will see your juicy black pussy." Jimmy whispered in her ear before he stood up and left the bar.

Chante was rooted to the spot. Her heart hammered wildly in her chest. She couldn't breathe as she dropped a few bills on the counter and finally stumbled her way out the exit.

"What have I done…" she whispered horrified.

She tried to remember as much detail of that particular night and realized her memory was too hazy. Jimmy must have known she never took drugs in all her life. No wonder she passed out cold. But the humiliation of just how low she had sunk filled her entire being.

She shivered as she made her way home. She couldn't open the door with her key. Her hand shook violently. She controlled the shiver that was engulfing her before she finally opened the lock. Once the door closed behind her, she felt an overwhelming sense of relief. At least she was safe inside her house.

Then just as suddenly, the enormity of her predicament struck her once more and she fell to the floor in a slump. Who could she turn too? She had no family except for Markey. She had no savings except for the salary she got as CNA and that wasn't much. It barely covered the rent and the groceries.

And even if she could get her hands on some money, will Jimmy hand over the video and forget everything?

Her brain shouted the truth of her predicament. There was no way Jimmy will ever be satisfied no matter how much money she could raise. He will use that to keep tormenting her until his attention shifted to something else.

Then what? A few weeks… or months later… before he shows up again? She could spend her whole life just being terribly afraid of him showing up again.

The hopelessness of her situation engulfed her once more. She had never felt more vulnerable and helpless her whole life. She cringed at the thought of the whole hospital finding out about her.

"Oh God…" Chante said in desperation.

Tears of helplessness and despair poured down her cheeks. She wished the ground would open up and swallow her whole. She had never felt more alone. Just when life was throwing her bits and pieces of hope, a dark past which she never expected have come to haunt her.

She struggled slowly to her feet and made her way to the bathroom. She felt an overwhelming desire to clean herself. She never felt so dirty in her entire life. Without even bothering to remove her clothes, she turned the shower on and stepped into the cold water. Her hair was wet and her drenched clothes stuck to her skin. But she knew that no matter how long she stayed inside the shower, it will never fully wash away the truth that she spent that one night in the arms of a scum bug like Jimmy Derollo.

Chapter Two

Chante forced her exhausted body out of bed the next morning. Dawn had broken the nighttime sky before heavy lids finally closed over tired eyes. She knew they would be red from crying, but there was nothing she could do about that now. She just hoped her brother wouldn't notice. She spent the whole night tossing and turning and thinking of a way out of her predicament.

Nothing proved to be the right solution. She knew that no matter where she went with this one Jimmy would always have the upper hand. He had the video and could extort money from her for as long as she lived.

She thought of moving away to escape him, but where would she go? Markey needed to be near a medical facility 24/7. And she was enrolled at the Community College and her tuition paid in full. If she suddenly disappeared, the hospital will definitely conduct a search. No…she had to stay and face the consequences.

She hoped and prayed that Jimmy would give her more time than the three days he threatened her with.

Chante felt the tears well in her eyes but she blinked them away. She couldn't afford to be weak. Not now…she needed to prepare Markey some breakfast and get ready for work.

She trudge into the kitchen in her bathrobe and realized that her brother was already up and in the living room watching cartoons.

"…morning," Markey greeted her.

"Hey…" Chante answered feebly.

She tried to keep her back to him so he wouldn't notice her red-rimmed eyes.

"What's wrong, Chant…" Markey inquired.

Chante didn't even realize he had wheeled himself from the living room and into the kitchen.

"What... oh… nothing… just a bad night, I guess." Chante evaded.

Markey said nothing but continued to watch her. Chante knew just how perceptive her brother was. She didn't want him to worry. She took in a deep breath and tried to put a huge smile on her face as she scooped some eggs and bacon onto his plate.

"Want some cereal to go with that?" She asked in a lighter voice.

Markey shook his head and started to eat. Chante poured herself a cup of coffee which she intended to bring back to the bedroom with her. She didn't want to sit at the breakfast table with him. She couldn't stand the thought of him seeing just how deeply troubled she was.

"Liza will be here shortly for your physical therapy," she announced to him.

"Ok…" Markey agreed and then added, "Chant, whatever it is, it'll be fine."

Chante was swept with an overwhelming desire to embrace him. She retraced her steps and placed her arms around him.

"Of course it will 'lil' bro…we will be fine. You and I both." Chante whispered in his ear.

Chante spent the next two days with her head in a swirling cloud of gray. It took all of her will to focus and concentrate on the things she had to do. She was glad that the hospital was full and she hardly had time to think about her situation. She moved about in a frenzy performing her duties, foregoing lunch, and she'd go straight home thoroughly exhausted and straight to bed.

She had formulated a plan. She would call Jimmy and ask to meet with him on the third day. Then she would beg him to give her some more time to come up with a substantial amount. If she needed to go down on her knees, she would. But the thought of seeing him again made her sick to the pit of her stomach. But that plan was the most she could come up with.

As the third day wore on, she found herself more and more nervous about what lie ahead. She realized that Jimmy would probably be waiting for her call and expecting that she had money with her. The thought made her nauseous. She ran to the toilet and slumped onto the bowl as bile regurgitated from the pit of her stomach. She heaved dryly. She hadn't eaten in almost three days. She splashed cold water onto her face and hoped that she looked none the worst for what was ahead.

As she trudged resignedly back to the nurses' station, she heard Nurse Betty call out her name. She held a stack of folders in her hand which she deposited into a satchel.

"Chante, I need you to bring this to…what's wrong? You look like you went through a meat grinder," Nurse Betty declared as she got a closer look at Chante's face.

"Bum stomach…" Chante lied.

"Are you alright?" the supervisor asked with concern.

"Yeah…I'll be fine…" Chante whispered weakly.

"OK…as I was saying, I need you to bring these documents to The Plaza. Mr. Lowell needs them ASAP," Nurse Betty informed her.

Mr. Lowell? Chante's senses fired up at the name. Jared Lowell? Was he back in New York?

Chante's equilibrium was sliced in half. Her heart managed to crawl out of its dark hole and celebrated the notion of seeing him again while her brain remained adamant, reminding her of Jimmy Derollo.

She took the satchel and reassured her supervisor that she knew where the plaza was. It was near Central Park and the streets were lined with recreational facilities and the boutique shops on Fifth and Madison Avenues.

When she reached the hotel, she headed straight to the reception area and asked to be directed to Mr. Lowell's room.

"It's the penthouse, Miss," the receptionist informed her with a look that said, 'did you really have to ask?'

"Of course it had to be the penthouse…" Chante mumbled to herself.

She glanced at her wrist watch and saw that it was 6:55 p.m. She would drop off the satchel and leave. The sooner she made contact with Jimmy the better. She didn't have any idea how he would accept her appeal, asking for a few days more.

The thought left her without sensation, foreshadowing whatever excitement she felt about seeing Jared again.

The elevator silently whisked her all the way to the top of The Plaza. She stepped out when it came to a stop and headed for the suite. She knocked at the Oakwood paneling of the Deluxe Rose Suite.

Jared opened the door and once again Chante was awestruck by the stunning beauty of the man. He must have just taken a shower because his hair appeared damp and disheveled. He was wearing a faded pair of Levi jeans and was shirtless. The six-pack rippled and glistened with moisture. The guy obviously had no need for a towel.

His brows knitted together and Chante thought he was not pleased to see her at all.

"Hi Jared…" Chante murmured as she awkwardly reached out her hand to pass on the satchel.

She averted her eyes from his half-naked body. She had no intentions of staying long or she would lose her mind completely.

"Chante…," his husky voice murmured her name, "Come in, please."

"I-err-I-I-can't s-s-stay…" Chante stuttered as Jared moved closer.

Chante stepped out of his way to avoid brushing against him as he closed the door behind her.

She expected the room to be pleasant but it was more breathtaking than she expected. The myriad lights of the New York skyline reflected against the glass windows of the living room.

Chante wondered why she always felt gauche in his presence. She felt like she had four sets of arms and legs and didn't know which limb to move first. She stayed rooted at the threshold as Jared sauntered towards the settee in the center of the room.

Chante prodded her feet to move forward. It seemed she had no choice except to stay a little while longer. She still held the satchel in her hand as she approached nearer.

"Nurse Betty said you needed this…so here…," Chante said placing the bag full of documents onto the table.

Jared sat down and gestured for her to do the same. He hadn't said another word since opening the door and the silence was starting to feel awkward. If Chante hadn't been so blinded by him, she would have noticed how his eyes lit up seeing her again. But it was her drawn and haggard face that immediately caught his attention.

Chante sat down tentatively only to rise again like her ass was on fire. She didn't want to inflict her presence on him.

"Sit down…," Jared ordered her softly.

There was no denying the command behind the softly spoken words. Chante sat down once again feeling like a marionette on strings. She clasped and unclasped her fingers and kept her eyes focused on her hands.

"Look at me…," Jared commanded once again.

Chante was compelled to obey. Emerald-green eyes locked with cobalt-blue ones.

"What's wrong," Jared asked softly this time. "You look like shit. Is that doctor of yours giving you trouble?"

"What?! Leo??? No-no-no…it's not about him…" Chante answered hastily.

"Your brother then…" Jared asked immediately.

"Markey? No-no-Markey is fine." Chante replied.

"Work?" Jared continued.

"No." Chante answered.

"Are we going to play 'Twenty Questions' or are you going to tell me what's wrong with you?" Jared sighed with exasperation.

Chante knew that Jared wouldn't stop until he flushed the truth out of her. But how could she even tell him about Jimmy and his extortion scheme? That video was the most horrifying thing that had ever happened to her and she had no intention of letting him know just how low she had sunk in the past.

Jared stared at her and saw the conflicting emotions pass through her face. He knew she was in some kind of trouble. Just as he knew it was something she was reluctant to share with him.

"Chante, listen…I know something's wrong. And obviously you are carrying this alone. You've lost a lot of weight. I see that. Let me help you…please. Whatever it is, I'm sure there's something I can do," Jared pleaded.

Chante was taken aback by the impassioned plea. She never in her wildest dreams considered Jared a shoulder to cry on. But the enormity of her burden during the last three days was suddenly too much to bear. Her shoulder slumped against the cushion as tears came rushing to her eyes. And like a dam that had been filled to overflowing, her sobs racked her body as her breath rattled against her throat.

"Hey…hey…hey…it's alright…," Jared said softly as he moved close beside her on the sofa and placed an arm across her shoulder.

Despite her distress, Chante was keenly aware of the fresh smell that permeated his body.

"No Jared, it's not alright…," She said between sobs.

Then she told him the truth. She kept nothing back. She shared with him about the lonely days after her mom passed away. Her confusion and fear about Markey. She told him about meeting Jimmy Derollo and the night he brought her to his apartment. And finally her humiliation over the video that Jimmy Derollo threatened to upload unless she came up with money tonight.

Throughout it all, Jared listened without saying a word. The only visible sign of his fury was a clenched jaw and the arm that tightened around Chante's shoulder.

"Are you… are you disgusted with me?" Chante asked in a hoarse voice.

Jared responded by taking her gently into his arms.

"Disgusted? No. Absolutely not. You were confused, lonely and scared and this bastard took advantage of you," Jared replied.

Chante nestled gently in his embrace. It felt so good to be in his arms. There was no other place she would rather be right this minute but she had to see Jimmy tonight and beg for an extension. She struggled out of his embrace, feeling immediately bereft, like coming from a warm bed and out into the cold.

"You're not going out to meet him tonight…I will," Jared said.

"But…," Chante replied confused.

"Give him a call. Tell him to meet you at the same bar and that you have the money with you. DO IT NOW!" Jared ordered her.

Chante was still confused but was compelled to do as he asked. When Jared spoke that way, she doubted anyone would ever try to cross him. Not even his mother.

Chante made the call as Jared threw on a shirt and a jacket.

"Stay here…wait for me till I get back…" Jared said quietly.

Chante was afraid of the look in his eyes. It had taken the color of an angry sea. His voice had a steely edge she'd never heard before.

"Jared, he might hurt you...," Chante protested as she clung to his arm in an attempt to stop him from leaving.

Jared grasped both her hands that were clinging tightly and held them in his own.

"I'll be fine, Chante. Stay here. I'll be back soon." Jared said before heading out the door.

After Jared left, Chante was collapsed in anger and desperation. She wanted to run after him, stop him from going to the bar. This was all so bad, she thought. The feeling of foreboding was so strong. And it was all her fault.

What she had done was manage to send Jared out to face an unknown danger. She should be the one out there, not him. This was her problem, not his. She never expected his reaction to be so quick.

"I should never have told him…," she thought.

"What if he gets hurt…or God forbid, even killed by Jimmy?" Chante muttered in agony.

How could she face his family? His mom…and dad…or girlfriend.

"Does he have a girlfriend?" Chante was momentarily sidetracked from her worry.

"He's been gone for so long...," Chante continued with her soliloquy.

She glanced at her watch and realized he had just been gone for twenty minutes and yet it felt like a lifetime.

She paced the floor, and then sat down on the sofa, only to jump up once more and continue with her pacing. She hardly noticed the plush surrounding, the rich texture of the upholstery on the chairs, the thick carpet on the floor, the luxurious colors on the wall, the fresh flowers strewn about the niches and crannies, and the beautiful artwork that hung all around the suite.

She hardly noticed any of these details yet the whole place screamed of the personality and character of someone like Jared Lowell. This place was who he was. A far cry from her reality-penniless… a sick brother… struggling to make ends meet.

Who was she to him? An accidental fuck brought about by circumstances of her making? Would he have given her a second look back at his mom's hospital room if she didn't challenge his machismo? Taunting him to kiss her so she could tell the nurses what a lousy kisser he was?

She remembered his proposition up on the roof deck and the pain she felt. It wasn't because she thought he treated her like a whore... offering her material comforts that she could only dream of. No…it wasn't that.

Chante now recognized the reason. It was because she believed in the fairytale ending. The happily ever after from books she read as a child. She always did. She wanted him to offer her more than just the luxuries that came with his fortune, or her being his kept woman…his sex toy. She wanted everything… heart, body, mind, and spirit. They could live in a shoebox and she'd be happy just to be with him. She wanted his promise of forever.

With all these thoughts running through her mind, Chante was suddenly struck with excruciating terror. What if she never saw him again after tonight? If something happened to him out there, she wouldn't be able to live with herself. Tears welled up in her eyes once again. She felt an icy coldness creep from her heart and envelop her entire body as she shivered violently.

If she could only turn back the hands of time, she would. It had been hours since he was gone.

She was so wrapped up in her desolation she hardly noticed the main door open silently.

"Chante…" Jared called out her name.

Chante stopped pacing and turned to where she heard his voice. She thought she was dreaming, her mind on overdrive. But no…it really was him, standing by the threshold.

"Jared?" she declared in a breathy unbelieving voice, still unsure if she was hallucinating.

Her knees turned to jelly as total desolation changed to encompassing relief. She swayed as the room spun around her.

From the corner of her eye she saw Jared take three large steps and caught her just before she lost her balance completely.

"Jared…oh God. Jared…you're back… you're back…thank God, you're back…" she cried out.

Without letting go of her, Jared led her to the sofa and sat down beside her.

Chante felt the need for reassurance that it was really him. She reached out her hand and touched his face.

"It's you…it's really you..," she muttered incoherently.

"Of course it's really me…unless you're expecting some else… then I can go…" Jared said seriously but the twinkle in his eyes belied the words.

The sound of his voice cleared all the cobwebs in her head. She had never felt more exhilarated and alive in her whole life. Jared was back.

And then Chante remembered why he left in the first place.

"What…how…did you…are you…?" the surge of questions rushing to her brain made the words difficult to form.

"If you promise me you're alright, then I'll tell you everything," Jared said calmly.

Chante nodded her head. She needed to keep calm if she were to get the whole story.

Jared took a deep breath and said, "I went to bar and waited for him. I didn't have to wait long. I recognized the scum bug the moment he entered. I asked him if he was waiting for you. He looked at me in surprise and said yes. I said you weren't coming and that I wanted something that he shouldn't have. And he gave it to me."

Jared reached into his pocket and drew out two objects.

"That's the hard drive to his computer and the memory card to his cell phone. Destroy it. And he promised never to get even remotely close to you again," Jared ended coolly.

Chante's eyes were wide as saucers. She couldn't believe what she was hearing. No way did things just happen the way he narrated it. There had to be more to it than that. She knew Jimmy Derollo… knew how mean and violent he could be. Jared wasn't telling her everything. She just knew it.

"Jar…," she began to protest.

But Jared placed a finger to her lips to stop her from asking more questions. He wasn't going to tell her anything more. She got that.

"That's all you need to know, Chante," Jared said firmly.

Chante slumped back into the backrest of the sofa. She couldn't believe her luck. The days of torment were over for her. Just like that. Then she remembered something. Her face suffused in shame and embarrassment.

"Did you see...," she couldn't even finish her sentence, the humiliation was overwhelming.

"No…I didn't want to. It's something personal that happened in your past," Jared answered with understanding.

Chante felt like she was submerged in cool cleansing water. She felt reborn and new. He gave her a new lease on the future. She didn't have to leave town, she didn't have to hide from anyone… her slate had been erased clean and it was all because of him.

Chante was filled with new hope. How could she ever repay him? There was no way she could ever equal what he had just given her tonight. He gave her back her life.

She raised her head up to give him a peck on the cheek. He was so close that all she had to do was inch her face forward. But Jared wasn't expecting that and turned towards her. And at that precise moment her kiss landed on his lips.

Jared stiffened at the unexpected intimacy. His adrenalin was still pumping. There was a lot he didn't tell Chante. He wanted to spare her the ugly details. But the unexpected feel of her lips on his unleashed all the pent-up control that built up since his encounter with Jimmy.

He pulled her close, and then even closer. His arms entwined around her waist with a viselike grip. Chante's arms snaked around his neck, her lips parting to allow his tongue entry. She felt his body emanating with a heat that burned and urged her to abandon all restraint.

Jared scooped her from off the sofa and carried her into the bedroom. Chante's heart was beating wildly, mesmerized by the thought of what was ahead. Chante knew she wouldn't hesitate. Not this time. This is what she wanted and her compliant body told him that.

Jared positioned her on the floor, their lips still pressed together, unable to let go. His fingers and palms were kneading and caressing her back as she felt the friction through the flimsy material of her clothes.

"Let me see all of you." Jared commanded.

And like a machine that animated under its master's power, Chante obeyed.

First she pulled out the barrette that was holding her hair and allowed it to fall softly against her shoulders. Her fingers moved and hovered tantalizingly on the hem of her blouse before she began to raise it up and over her head. Then she unzipped her pants and allowed them to drop carelessly around her ankles before kicking them aside. She stood before him naked except for her undies.

Jared's eyes drank in the tawny sheen of her light chocolate skin, the full breasts that begged to be set free from its confines, the narrow waist that angled softly to ample hips. He looked at her face and saw how her eyes dilated with desire, her lips parted, her breathing shallow.

He stepped closer and reached behind to unclasp her bra, setting free nipples that puckered hard with her lust. Chante shimmied out of her panties, exposing a trimmed bush of pubes.

He cupped both of her breasts, running his palms over the hard nipples, gently holding them in his hands. Her skin was as incredibly silky and soft as it looked, yielding instantly to his strokes, giving way to his insistent caresses. He kept stroking her, bringing his hands to the flat belly, and then to her back, sensing her shiver each time his fingers reached the firm swell of her ass, her breathing becoming more and more abandoned.

Jared brought her to the bed, slow, gently. He had to exert control not to fuck her there and then. He wanted this to be a slow dance, unlike their frenetic mating the first time they met.

Chante was bemused, dazed, her whole body ablaze. Her brain, which had detached from her body, watched in rapt attention as Jared removed all his clothes. She couldn't take her eyes off the throbbing cock that reared up with a life of its own. The thin skin on his cock shone with a pinkish hue while the head was suffused in a darker shade of crimson.

She was bewildered as he positioned her arms towards the back of the bed and pulled her body down near the edge of the bed. He spread her knees apart and guided one leg so that one foot was firmly planted on the floor.

Jared bent his head before her open thighs and felt the warmth even before he touched her. He parted the lips of her pussy, blowing gently against her clit, caressing them with his breath. Then his tongue reached out and began kissing her there. Chante moaned as her back arched with the anticipated pleasure. Jared gently kissing her clit was beyond her wildest imagination. She thought she had reached the zenith of her pleasure until he began sucking her. Chante bucked wildly as bolts of blue fire went shooting through her entire body.

She was already wet when they started kissing and now her juices were flowing freely from her pussy. Jared slipped a finger inside her, keeping his tongue firmly sucking on her clit. Chante thought she would surely go insane. She was moaning loudly, her back arched from the bed, her fingers clawing wildly at the headboard.

She wanted him to stop or else she would lose her mind as his fingers twirled inside her and his relentless tongue tortured her swollen clit. The muscles deep inside her vagina clenched around his finger desperately wanting his cock more than anything in the world but still unable to let go.

Chante was moaning as her body was racked with torturous hot and cold sensations. She didn't want to cum in his mouth and her hands groped wildly through his hair. But she knew she was losing all control of her body. She bucked wildly as Jared slowed down the circling motion of his tongue against her clit only to pick up speed once more, drawing her further away from the little that was left of her self-control. She felt her vagina spasm as she let out a keening cry of pleasure. Her body shook in one final arch before she collapsed onto the bed unable to contain her orgasm.

"Jared, I'm so sorry," Chante uttered breathlessly.

But Jared scrambled onto the bed and flipped her over. He pulled her by the hips until she was kneeling on the bed with her ass up in the air. Chante felt the head of his cock probing the opening of her ass before sliding down and entering her pussy from behind.

Jared reached out and cupped her breast, his thumb and forefinger twirling against her sensitive nipples. Chante realized the tension was building up once again inside her. Jared thrust into her slowly as his hands traveled down to her engorged clitoris. Chante almost jumped as a warm current passed through her whole body.

Her own cum had made her so slick that Jared had an easy time rubbing both sides of her hood between his fingers. He rubbed her slowly and then with ever increasing intensity as his thrust grew harder and stronger. Chante felt her orgasm building inside again. And as she climbed higher and higher into her own release, she heard Jared grunt like an animal in heat before she felt her own body start to shake. With one

final thrust Jared came inside her as the muscles inside
her cunt clenched violently before following with her
own cum.

Chapter Three

In a seedy part of Queens, decrepit and broken-down warehouses lined an alley littered with garbage. Trash vats lay strewn all over the narrow cobblestone as rats scurried in and out of open bins in search of food scraps. A stench of death and decay filled the air.

One particular building had its door pried open. The marks of a crowbar were visible against the door jamb as the doorknob lay teetering and dented against the door.

A flight of stairs led to the second floor of the building where floorboards were broken and knawed away in several places. Rat droppings littered everywhere. A slight breeze blew against a torn and dirty curtain hanging by a glass pane, remnants of its shattered glass sticking out of the edges of the window sill.

A broken couch with its spiral coils showing through the tattered upholstery was positioned against the window. Whatever little light filtered through the glass was obscured by cigarette smoke that hung heavily in the air.

A stooped figure limped painfully towards the couch in small measured steps. Any abrupt movement

triggered spasms of pain from his broken ribs. His
entire body throbbed. He reached the sofa and lowered
his ass down slowly. A neoprene wrist pad covered his
left hand. He tried flexing his fingers to gauge the
damage on the muscles and was instantly rewarded by a
stab of pain that reached all the way to his elbow.

"Fuck…" Jimmy Derollo grimaced in pain.

He had been hiding in this dump for the last twenty
four hours. He couldn't show himself back in the old
neighborhood. The bruises on his face and neck would
be a dead giveaway. Someone may just think of calling
his parole officer, and then shit would hit the fan, that's
for sure.

No…he'd burrow his broken body here in this
dump and wait until he felt better. He had all the time in
the world. His stash of crack cocaine and a bottle of
brandy lay at the foot of the sofa. That should get him
through for the next few days.

He remembered last night and what happened. He
was waiting for Chante at the bar when this stranger
came to him. He said that Chante was outside in his car
with the money Jimmy needed. The guy opened the
side of a black SUV and shoved him in. The next thing
Jimmy knew he was punched kicked and pummeled to
the floor of the car. He was beaten to within an inch of
his life. Jimmy begged for mercy saying he had some
money in his pocket and the man could have everything
he wanted.

The guy smashed his head against the floor of the
SUV and said that all he needed was the video he had

of Chante. Jimmy got a clearer glimpse of his face. He thought he recognized the face but couldn't put a name to it. But it was the eyes that drove Jimmy to terror. There was a look of murderous rage in them. Jimmy knew that if he didn't do as told, the stranger wouldn't have second thoughts ending Jimmy's miserable life.

Jimmy cowered in fear as he took his cell phone from his back pocket. The man removed the memory card and erased the video. Next they took a small drive to Jimmy's apartment where the man smashed his laptop and removed the hard drive from within.

Before he drove away the man hissed a message into his ear, "If you ever come near her again, I swear to God, no one will ever find your body," the guy threatened in a menacing voice.

Jimmy didn't even realize he pissed his pants till the car was out of sight. He went back into his apartment, gathered a few things and left quickly before the pain hit him hard.

Jimmy reached out for his stash and spread some white stuff on a piece of broken glass pane he retrieved from the window. He snorted hard and waited for the anesthetic effect to remove some of the pain. He took a swig from the brandy. With some of the pain gone, Jimmy managed to gather some coherent thoughts.

"That fucking bitch…this is all her doing… managed to hire a thug… paid money to get the video back. But how? She claimed to have no money… even fucking begged me not to do it. That guy…he looked familiar…not the kind of thug who'd do this for cash. I know him…I've seen him somewhere before." Jimmy sorted through his fogged brain.

And then in a moment of clarity, Jimmy straightened, triggering his broken ribs to press hard against his chest muscle.

"Awww…," Jimmy cried in pain.

"The Village Voice," Jimmy suddenly remembered a local newspaper, "some kind of announcement about a fucking director for NY General Hospital."

"Gareth…Jeric…Jared Lowell…that's it. That's the guy from last night. Fucking Jared Lowell, head of Lowell Enterprise. Well…well…well, looks like my Chante had gotten herself some fancy fuck." Jimmy said.

The pain wracking his body burned into slow anger. Jimmy fueled the anger by snorting more cocaine until the combined effects with the alcohol produced a blind rage. He forgot that he was under parole as a plan slowly formed in his head. When the scenario was executed perfectly in his mind, he slumped back slowly onto the sofa and closed his eyes.

A sinister smile marked his face as he muttered into the darkness, "We shall meet again Chante Green. And when we do, my face will be the last image you will ever see."

Chapter Four

Chante stepped down from the curb in front of the café. She refused to look back. She knew that the silhouette of Leo Cadman would be visible even from outside. His dejection was hard to bear. But Chante knew she did the right thing.

She determined that breaking up with Leo would be difficult. But it was harder to live with the guilt that hounded her every single day. Ever since the night she spent in the arms of Jared, she knew this time would come.

But she was wracked with uncertainty as well and that was not something she wanted Leo to see. When Leo asked her why, she didn't know how exactly to answer the question. But Leo was intuitive and when he asked if there was someone else, Chante nodded her head indicating he was right.

Chante was glad he didn't ask who. Her ambiguity rose from the fact that she didn't know where she stood with Jared. The time they spent together was something that she will forever remember, if memories were all that she would have. When she left that morning, Jared was still sleeping. She hurriedly scribbled a note thanking him for everything he had done for her.

Breaking up with Leo meant she had just blown her chances for a stable future beside a promising doctor and a man who obviously adored her. Chante had to convince herself that this decision had nothing to do with Jared. Whether he was in her life or not, she had to do the right thing. She wasn't in love with Leo, and that was the hard truth.

Jared had called her a couple of times since that night but Chante refused to take any of his calls. She was determined to set things straight with Leo before she even came near Jared again. She didn't want her conscience compounded with guilt of cheating on Leo every time she came near the presence of Jared Lowell.

But now it was done and Chante felt liberated for the first time since she accepted Leo's proposal. She wanted to call Jared but her insecurity about everything concerning him was brought to the forefront once again. She decided to wait for his next call…if he will ever call her again.

Her phone rang and Chante's heart leapt to her throat.

"Hey, Chant…," she recognized her brother's voice on the line

"Markey…is something wrong?" Chante asked trying to hide the disappointment in her voice.

"Nah…just wanted to say that you had a visitor a few minutes ago. He had the most awesome car. T'was a Benz. It had the most awesome panoramic glass roof.

He took me driving around the block." Markey said with obvious excitement in his voice.

"WHAT??? You went driving with someone I don't know about?" Chante asked with horror in her voice.

"Well, he said you were a good friend. And he looked good. You know…real rich and all that stuff." Markey replied with a hint of regret.

"Besides, Liza said it was alright. I mean…she was all ruffled and confused and didn't know how to act around him. She was all red in the face like she was on fire or sumthin…" Markey informed her.

Chante knew that Markey was trying to deflect the attention from what he did. But a twinge of excitement began to bloom in her stomach.

"Did-did he say who he was?" Chante asked.

"Uhmm…said his name was Jared Lowell and that he works in the same hospital you do. That's why I thought it was ok. Are you mad at me for driving with him? T'was really cool…you know," Markey posed with some hesitation.

"Yeah…yeah…it's alright Markey. But don't you ever do that again without telling me first," Chante reprimanded her brother.

"Okay," Markey replied, "but Jared said that he's been calling you and you don't pick up the phone. So he looked up where you lived and all that stuff." Markey informed her.

"Did… did Jared say where I can find him?" Chante asked trying to hide the excitement in her voice.

"Yup…said he was goin' back to the hospital…" Markey answered.

Chante hung up the phone and hailed a passing cab. She wanted to get to Jared fast. If she had wings she'd probably be floating on air right now. Surely, him coming to her house… looking for her meant something. And he'd been calling her too.

The excitement in the pit of her stomach started to bloom. For some strange reason she felt exhilarated, euphoric, expectant. She was going to see him again. She told the cabbie to proceed to NY General as she sat back and tried to contain her excitement. She whipped out her compact mirror and stared at her reflection. Her eyes were luminous and her face was flushed. She hardly noticed the passing scenery, mentally urging the cab to go even faster. She breathed a sigh of relief as they turned a corner leading to the entrance of NY General.

She almost jumped out of the cab in her rush to see him. And she did. He was coming from the opposite direction. The disheveled hair flying in the breeze, the long strides of powerfully built legs wrapped in denim jeans, the white shirt with the sleeves rolled all the way to his elbow… all these images stamped their mark in Chante's psyche. His head was bowed as if he carried the world on his shoulders. Chante could see clearly the glumness that creased his face.

"Jared…," Chante called out.

Chante immediately saw the transformation on his face. He looked at her from afar like she was everything he wanted to see. The glumness gave way to relief that was followed by a smile of pure joy.

Chante ran to him like the devil was after her. She wanted to feel his arms around her… she wanted him to kiss her. She came to a full stop when she was right in front of him, suddenly feeling shy. She had to restrain herself. The lobby was full of bystanders and it was broad daylight.

They stood there in the sunlight. Jared's hands clasped her upper arms, her hands on his chest. They drank in the sight of each other. Their eyes devoured each other. Chante saw when Jared looked up past her head like something caught his attention. The silly grin that was on his face vanished and was replaced by surprise that suddenly turned into one of horror.

She swiveled her head halfway to see. And then she heard the voice.

"Bitch and your man-whore….," the slurred voice of Jimmy Derollo reached her ear.

Chante couldn't remember what happened next. Everything was a blur. She felt Jared yank her hard to the side and away just as two gunshots filled the air.

Pandemonium broke loose. People scampered everywhere. Screams filled the air. Chante thought she saw everything in slow motion… hospital security police rushing out and pinning Jimmy to the ground. The wail of a siren blared in the distance.

Chante looked at Jared and saw that the front of his shirt was stained with a crimson color. Blood…blood…was the thought that came rushing into Chante's mind.

Jared tottered and Chante grabbed him just before he collapsed onto the ground.

"NO…GOD…JARED… NO!!! Chante recalled screaming at the top of her voice.

Jared reached out a bloodied hand to touch her face.

"I love you, Chante," he whispered before he slumped against her chest.

Chapter Five

The hours that followed the shooting of Jared Lowell were a blur in Chante's mind. Emergency personnel, doctors and nurses came rushing out of the hospital in droves. A trolley was speedily brought out from the emergency door as a mob of white-coated medics followed in hot pursuit. Instructions were shouted by a doctor and carried out by nurses before Jared was whisked back inside the hospital.

Chante stood numbed with shock. Her whole body had turned cold. She couldn't stop crying and screaming Jared's name. Nurse Betty and some of the other nurses from the second floor came and tried to calm her down. She felt a prick on her arm and realized she was injected with a sedative.

But she didn't want to go to sleep. She had to go and see what was happening with him.

"It's alright, honey, it's just for you to calm down." Nurse Betty declared.

Chante insisted on being brought to the ER. She almost got away from them before Nurse Betty got hold of her and told her she couldn't do that. Jared was being prepped for surgery.

She calmed down long enough for them to accompany her to the waiting room. That was the most they could do for her but Nurse Betty promised to get back to her as soon as they heard any news.

Chante was relieved the waiting room was almost empty. She wanted to be alone with her thoughts. She was exhausted from crying. She felt so helpless and so alone.

The door opened and Chante was surprised to see Leo come in. She left him at the café. She glanced at her watch and realized that was hours ago.

"Leo…" Chante cried out haltingly.

Leo saw how totally distraught she was.

"Is he the one, Chante?" Leo asked simply.

Chante realized that word must have gotten around by now. She was with Jared when he got shot. It was in her arms where he collapsed. Talk was rife in a hospital setting and people would make their conclusions whether she liked it or not. The nurses were all probably gossiping about her now and her relationship with Jared Lowell.

Chante remembered how Jared reached for her face and tenderly caressed her cheek before he lost consciousness. The last words he uttered were forever imprinted in her heart.

'I love you, Chante,' she recalled.

Remembering those words triggered a fresh deluge of tears. Her shoulders heaved as she tried to control the surge of her emotions. She was worried sick about him now but Leo needed an answer.

"Yes...," Chante replied.

Leo held her at arm's length and said, "Don't worry...we'll do everything we can to save him."

Then he left.

Chante realized the irony of her situation. She broke up with a man she did not love and now she had to trust that man to save the one she loved.

Chante didn't know how long she sat there before the police came and took her statement. They confirmed what she knew and what the other witnesses saw. Jared pushed her out of harm's way and took the bullet instead.

After they had gone, the door opened once again and Mrs. Samantha Lowell entered the waiting room. She was exactly as Chante remembered her last. Patrician, cool, and collected even if her eyes were red-rimmed with tears.

She approached Chante with arms opened wide. Chante received her embrace and sobbed once again.

"It's all my fault...it should have been me...,"she cried with muffled sobs.

"Then you don't know Jared the way I do. He will protect anyone he loves even if it means putting his own life in danger." Samantha Lowell said.

They both sat down, arms entwined around each other. Somehow Mrs. Lowell knew. Chante didn't know if Jared told her anything about them. Most probably not. But Mrs. Lowell didn't seem the type of woman who would be the last to know.

The room filled up with visitors as the hours ticked by. Chante recognized some of the ranking members of the hospital board. Lawyers, bankers, political luminaries, and well-known media personalities came and made a beeline for Samantha Lowell. Chante marveled at the dignity in which Mrs. Lowell graciously accepted their concern.

Refreshments were brought in, people milled around in small groups, and despite the somber mood, Chante was glad Mrs. Lowell had her friends about.

She tried to make herself as inconspicuous as possible and was glad when Nurse Betty entered the room with some of the other nurses. She looked straight at Chante and shook her head, indicating there was no word yet about Jared's condition.

Chante wondered if she should stay or go. She wasn't family and she didn't want Samantha Lowell's friends to start wondering who she was and why she was here at all. But she was spared the indecision when the door opened and Dr. Leo Cadman entered the room. All eyes turned to him as he approached Mrs. Lowell. You could hear a pin drop with the silence that ensued.

Chante suppressed the urge to run to him for news. That wasn't her place. But she was filled with apprehension and moved forward as the rest of the people did. Leo searched for her face among the crowd that milled around him, saw her, smiled, and then addressed Mrs. Lowell.

"Mr. Lowell will be fine…," Leo announced as a small cheer erupted inside the room.

"We extracted the bullet that was lodged in his shoulder. The other bullet was a bit tricky as it fragmented near his upper right parietal pleura. We had to make sure all the fragments were removed." Leo announced.

"How… how… is he? Is he still sedated?" Mrs. Lowell asked.

Her scratchy voice was the only indication of the strain she must have been carrying since she found out about the shooting.

"Well…" Leo continued scratching his head, perplexed, and aggravated, "he's awake now. I wanted to give him a sedative to allow him to rest and recover. But he was adamant and refused. He said he was feeling fine."

"Oh thank God," Chante mumbled, staggering backward in relief.

Leo looked at Mrs. Lowell sheepishly and continued, "He's asking for…well…he's asking for…"

Leo glanced at Chante before turning back to Mrs. Lowell, "He's asking for you, ma'am."

"Bull crap...," Mrs. Lowell uttered as a few of the guests chuckled. "You don't have to spare this old lady's feelings. I know my son. As much as he would be happy to see me, he'd be happier now to see the woman he loves. He's asking for Chante Green, right?"

"Right...," Leo agreed without hesitation.

Chante heard her name echoed repeatedly across the room. Nurse Betty hugged her as another triumphant cheer erupted from the nurses around the room.

Samantha Lowell drew near and hugged her tightly before declaring for everyone to hear, "Go to him, Chante. Nurse that beautiful man of ours back to health."

And that was all the encouragement Chante needed. She approached Leo and embraced him before whispering a soft 'thank you' in his ear.

Then she walked towards the door as applause followed her every stride. And when she was outside in the hallway, she ran as fast as her feet could carry her. She felt light as a feather; her ankles sprouted unseen wings that carried her swiftly towards the man who held the promise of a glorious future in his hands.

-The End-

If you enjoyed this title, I would appreciate your leaving a review of the book. Good reviews encourage an author to write as well as help books to sell. Good reviews can be just a few short sentences describing what you liked about the book without having a spoiler. If you could spend 30 seconds writing a review, I would appreciate it: you can review this title right now at your favorite retailer.

Here is a preview of **another story** you may enjoy:

Suspicion: Elusive Billionaire Romance Series, Book 1

"**I WANT** to know who the hell is responsible for this mess!" boomed Hendrick from the front of the boardroom.

Silence filled the room as all the top people in the company stared at Hendrick in awe. They knew he wasn't the kind of guy to be messed with. Considering the company had just been charged with federal and criminal charges for dumping industrial waste into the Arctic Ocean, they knew it was best to stay silent.

"I return from vacation to find the prosecutor in my office to tell me that a company that I built from the ground up to help humanity is being accused of filling the ocean with waste! Waste??" He screamed across the table, his face turning an angry red. Hendrick stopped for a moment to compose himself and looked at each person at the table, assessing their worth.

"Pray it was not one of you frontrunners that made the decision to handle the waste of the company in this manner. Now go, and I expect reports hourly about how we are making this right and where waste should be going from now on."

Everyone got up from the table quickly and filtered out of the room. Hendrick watched them all leave and turned to his right-hand man, Geoffrey, the CEO of the company.

"Tell me you didn't know."

A broad-shouldered man, Geoffrey held an imposing frame that fit well with the red beard that made him appear like a Viking. He was incredibly loyal and a great asset to the company.

"You have known me your whole life Hendrick, I'm sure you know I had nothing to do with dumping waste into the ocean. The person in charge of a decision like that is one of your minions."

"How is it that the owner and CEO of a company had no idea that his own company has been poisoning the ocean?"

"Someone down the line obviously felt it would save the company a lot of money."

Hendrick snorted, "Ya and no one would ever find out that the Arctic Ocean was suddenly polluted? My god they have vessel numbers and everything, it was our guys to be sure, so how do I not know about it?"

"The prosecutors are doing their investigation and so are we. I can guarantee that we will find out who is responsible before anyone else does."

"I'm being prosecuted, Geoffrey! They think I knew about this madness."

"Look you didn't know and they can't prove that you did. You will have your day in court and they will simply have to let it go. They can't pull evidence from thin air so you're safe."

Hendrick went to the side table by the grand picture window. He poured them both a glass of bourbon, handing one to Geoffrey.

"I built this company because I believed in a vision and now our reputation is being smeared. All the while I'm off doing fundraisers and charity events while some asshole is destroying the ocean under my name."

If you enjoyed this sample then look for **Suspicion: Elusive Billionaire Romance Series, Book 1**.

Here is a preview of **another book** you may also enjoy:

Love Requited - Ardent Billionaire Romance Series, Book 3

"I'M SO proud of you Deirdre. Here's to a successful demo recording." Cassie smiled. Deirdre lifted her glass of champagne to her friend's toast.

"Brooke said it went really well," Deirdre told her friend. "She said we can expect a decision from the studio execs in the next week or so." Deirdre had spent all day recording what could turn into her first album. She'd been working for weeks, choosing songs that were perfectly suited for her strong soprano voice. This after recording dinner with Cassie was the first time she'd allowed herself to relax in six weeks.

"I just know they're going to sign you. You deserve something fantastic like this, Dee." Cassie smiled. "And just think of all of the things you'll be able to do for D'Angelo. You're going to be able to give him an amazing life."

An uncomfortable look spread across Deirdre's face. "Do you really think so? Felix is afraid that if I'm in the public eye, D'Angelo will suffer for it… I'm afraid he has a point. I mean, look at how most celebrity kids turn out. It's ridiculous… I'd never want that for my brother. I loved recording the demo, but maybe this isn't something I should pursue. Maybe I should just keep focusing on school and let D'Angelo have a quiet life." Deirdre sighed.

Cassie took a long sip of her champagne and studied her friend. "Do you really think that a little attention and money will be worse for D'Angelo than what he's already been through?" she asked firmly. Deirdre opened her mouth to respond, but Cassie kept plowing on. "He deserves the best, even more than you do. And you're a good person, Dee. You'll make sure he is too." She paused for another moment before continuing. "This doesn't sound like you, Deirdre. Whose idea was it for you to turn down the deal?"

Deirdre looked down before answering. "Felix just pointed out that fame can be fleeting. And leave lasting damage. I just don't know what the right thing is…"

"And Parker? I'm assuming you're still talking to him?" Cassie prodded.

Deirdre shook her head. "He's been keeping his distance. He sent flowers once… he's sent over food with notes, saying he's thinking about me, knows I'm busy. And he's been taking D'Angelo to ball games… but he always stays in the hallway… like he's literally giving me my space. He said he'd wait as long as it takes, I'm starting to think he meant it."

"Maybe I misjudged our handsome billionaire," Cassie conceded. "And maybe you should talk to him about your decision. Who would know better about the pros and cons of having enormous loads of money?" She laughed.

"I'd love to talk to him about this," Deirdre agreed, "but I'm not sure I can trust myself around Parker. The last time we were alone together, I almost cheated on Felix. He doesn't deserve that."

"Deirdre, it almost sounds like you're staying with Felix out of obligation. Aren't you the one who pointed out that he deserves better than that?" Cassie reminded her.

Deirdre sighed. "And aren't you the one who said I was allowed to take time?" She countered.

"Yes… but that was back when Felix seemed like a good fit for you. The longer you've stayed with him, the less I think that. He's discouraging you from taking advantage of a once in a lifetime opportunity… It almost sounds like he's intimidated by the idea of you succeeding."

"Felix loves D'Angelo,'" Deirdre snapped defensively. "He's just trying to make sure I put his needs first, that's all. You should see the two of them together, Cass. D'Angelo loves him. And Felix has a point; my decisions affect my brother as much as they affect me."

"It sounds like Felix wants you to put HIS needs first and he's hiding behind an eight year old," Cassie said firmly. She sighed. "We've gotten off track, Dee, tonight was supposed to be a celebration. Take the deal or don't take the deal, it doesn't change the fact that this is a pretty big honor. I'm proud of you." Cassie smiled.

"It is kinda a big honor, isn't it?" Deirdre smiled, allowing her friend to change the subject.

Cassie nodded. "And it could be the beginning of the rest of your life."

<<◇>>

Deirdre slowly unlocked her front door and gently pushed it open. She crept into the living room and found D'Angelo and Felix asleep on the couch, the menu screen of The Lion King shining from the television set. Deirdre kneeled down and shook Felix slightly.

"Hmm," he murmured, opening his eyes. "What time is it?"

"It's a little after eleven," Deirdre whispered. "Cassie and I didn't stay out long. I was ready to get home." She smiled, moving to D'Angelo's side of the couch. She leaned down and kissed him lightly all over the face. D'Angelo woke up laughing.

"How did the song making go Dee Dee?" he asked with bright eyes and a tired smile.

"The song making went great little man." She smiled. "I'll make you a deal. Go to your room and go back to sleep, and as soon as you wake up in the morning I'll tell you all about it."

"You promise?"

"Absolutely," Deirdre assured him. D'Angelo jumped up, hugged his sister and Felix, and then scampered off to his bed.

"He's such a good kid." Felix smiled. "So, it really went well?"

55

"It really did." Deirdre smiled. "But I'm still thinking about what you said. I'm not sure that kind of lifestyle is best for D'Angelo."

"Well, whether you accept a contract or not, this is a great honor Deirdre, you should be proud of yourself. I'm proud of you." He grinned.

Deirdre sat on Felix's lap, leaned over, and lightly nibbled his earlobe. "Wanna show me how proud?" she whispered suggestively.

"Always…" he said quickly before covering her mouth with his. Felix wrapped Deirdre's legs around his hips, stood, and carried her into the bedroom. He fell backward onto the bed, pulling away from Deirdre just long enough to pull her shirt over her head. Deirdre unhooked her bra and threw it aside and then shimmied out of her slacks. Felix took her right breast into his mouth roughly, biting and pinching her nipple until Deirdre burned with desire.

"Hey Felix, I've had a long day," Deirdre breathed heavily. "Would you care to take this to the shower?" She grinned mischievously.

"Always." he said again, returning her grin. Deirdre climbed off of Felix and shook her ass as she walked to her bathroom. Felix jumped from the bed, stripping off his clothes as he followed.

If you enjoyed this sample then look for **Love Requited - Ardent Billionaire Romance Series, Book 3.**

Here is a preview of **another book** you may also enjoy:

Love Decided - Lonely Billionaire Romance Series, Book 3

TRICIA WAITED impatiently at the door. Her hands were shaking with nervous tension. It had taken an unbelievable amount of time to do her makeup because her hands kept jerking as she tried to apply lipstick and mascara. Finally, it seemed like it was almost time for John to arrive. Trying to calm her nerves, she sat down on the couch.

Although it seemed like forever ago, Tricia had once been in love with John. Despite their better intentions, they had succumbed to an animalistic desire and had sex—more times than she could count. Tricia had been nursing his sick wife, Rebecca, until she died. After Rebecca's death, Tricia had returned home and taken care of her mother. Now, it seemed like anything was possible. After burying her mother, John had sent her a message and flowers for her birthday. She was going to have dinner with him tonight.

Tricia smoothed her dress awkwardly. She had worn this red dress not long before she had finally had sex with John for the first time. Although she had pretended not to notice, she had seen him watching her slim curves move and strain against the fabric. She cursed herself silently. How could she possibly be trying to dress up for him? Since Tricia had returned home, she had dated Rod. Attractive and successful, Rod was a wealthy real estate developer. More importantly, he was kind, funny and actually black. Although times were changing, dating someone of the same race would still make her life easier. Ruining things with Rod would be terrible. He was her best friend, Tenaya's, brother and she would probably lose her friend as well as her boyfriend.

Standing up, Tricia walked over to the phone. She wanted to call John and tell him that she could not make it. Being around John would be an impossible temptation for her. Dialing the phone number, she waited until his voicemail picked it up. Unwilling to cancel a date with a message, she went over to the couch to sit down again. Before she could get comfortable, she heard a knock at the door.

Groaning, she managed to smile before she pulled the door open. In front of her, John stood with a handful of red roses. Smiling widely, he made a move toward her and seemed prepared to sweep her off her feet in an instant. Pushing his hand away, she gave him a hug.

Confused, John hugged her before stepping back. "You look...ravishing, Tricia. How are you?" In his voice, she could hear the unspoken question. He did not know about Rod and could not understand her hesitation.

"I'm good, John. For a while, I was confused and depressed after my mother's death. Fortunately, Rod was there to help me through it." As soon as she said this, she regretted it. Tricia had wanted to slip Rod's name in so that John would know she had a boyfriend. John's crestfallen expression made her instantly reconsider this decision. "Here, come in, come in. I can get you a cup of tea or something before we go. Did you want anything?"

If you enjoyed this sample then look for **Love Decided - Lonely Billionaire Romance Series, Book 3**.

Other Books by Shyla Starr

- Persuasive Billionaire BWWM Romance Series

- Tenacious Billionaire BWWM Romance Series

- Elusive Billionaire Romance Series

- Lonely Billionaire Romance Series

- Ardent Billionaire Romance Series

- Fervent Billionaire BWWM Romance Series

Get the latest update on new releases from the author at:

https://shylastarr.com/newsletter/

About the Author - Shyla Starr

Shyla currently specializes in writing interracial romance stories and is a huge fan of the alpha male. Simply put, there just aren't enough stories about mixed couple romances, which is something she is aiming to fix.

Being a bookworm all her life, when Shyla discovered men she also realized how easy it was to fulfill her fantasies through her writing.

When not writing and fantasizing about men, Shyla enjoys dancing, reading and chilling with her friends.

Connect with Shyla Starr

I really appreciate you reading my book! Here are my social media coordinates:

Friend me on Facebook:
https://www.facebook.com/shylastarrauthor

Follow me on Twitter: https://twitter.com/shylstarr

Check me out on Goodreads:
https://www.goodreads.com/author/show/8436084.Shyl a_Starr

Subscribe to my newsletter:
https://shylastarr.com/newsletter/

Visit my website: https://shylastarr.com/